DATE DUE

OC 04 '89	AG 20 '91	MR 28 '94	OC 12 '96
NO 14 '89	OC -4 '91	MY 14 '94	DE 28 '96
NO 29 '89	OC 19 '91	JE 20 '94	MR 15 '97
MR 10 '90	JE 12 '92	JY 20 '94	JE 11 '97
MR 27 '90	JE 30 '92	JY 28 '94	JY 21 '97
AP 04 '90	JY 27 '92	AG 11 '94	MR 25 '98
JY 9 '90	SE 16 '92	OC 29 '94	JY 15
JY 13 '90	JY 6 '93	NO 15 '94	
SE 6 '90	JY 21 '93	NO 23 '94	DE 02 '10
DE 12 '90	AG 3 '93	DE 1 '94	
FE 18 '91	AG 24 '93	FE 4 '95	
MR 25 '91	SE 22 '93	JE 10 '95	
AP 15 '91		AG 9 '95	
MY 20 '91	OC 26 '93		
JE 26 '91	NO 11 '93	SE 7 '95	
		OC 17 '95	
JY 02 '91	DE 6 '93	JY 9 '96	
JY 16 '91	AP 14 '94	AG 24 '96	

DEMCO 38-297

Published in the United States by E. P. Dutton,
2 Park Avenue, New York, N.Y. 10016,
a division of NAL Penguin Inc.

Published simultaneously in Canada by
Fitzhenry & Whiteside Limited, Toronto

Designer: Barbara Powderly

Printed in Hong Kong by South China Printing Co.
First Edition   COBE   10 9 8 7 6 5 4 3 2 1

Library of Congress Cataloging-in-Publication Data

Stevenson, Robert Louis. 1850–1894.
Block City / by Robert Louis Stevenson; illustrated by
Ashley Wolff.—1st ed.
p.   cm.
Summary: A child creates a world of his own which has
mountains and sea, a city and ships, all from toy blocks.
ISBN 0-525-44399-1
I. Children's poetry, English.   [1. Blocks (Toys)—Poetry.
2. English poetry.]   I. Wolff, Ashley, ill.   II. Title.
PR5489.B55   1988   87-33397
821'.8—dc19   CIP
                                                        AC

ROBERT LOUIS STEVENSON

· · ·

BLOCK CITY

· · ·

illustrated by

ASHLEY WOLFF

E. P. DUTTON · NEW YORK

for my dear Brennan

What are you able to
build with your blocks?
Castles and palaces,
temples and docks.

Rain may keep raining,
and others go roam,

But I can be happy and building at home.

Let the sofa be mountains, the carpet be sea,

And a harbor as well where
my vessels may ride.

A kirk
and a mill
and a palace beside,

n the top of it all,
down in an orderly way
essels lie safe in the bay.

There I'll establish a city for me:

A sort of a tower o

And steps coming

To where my toy v

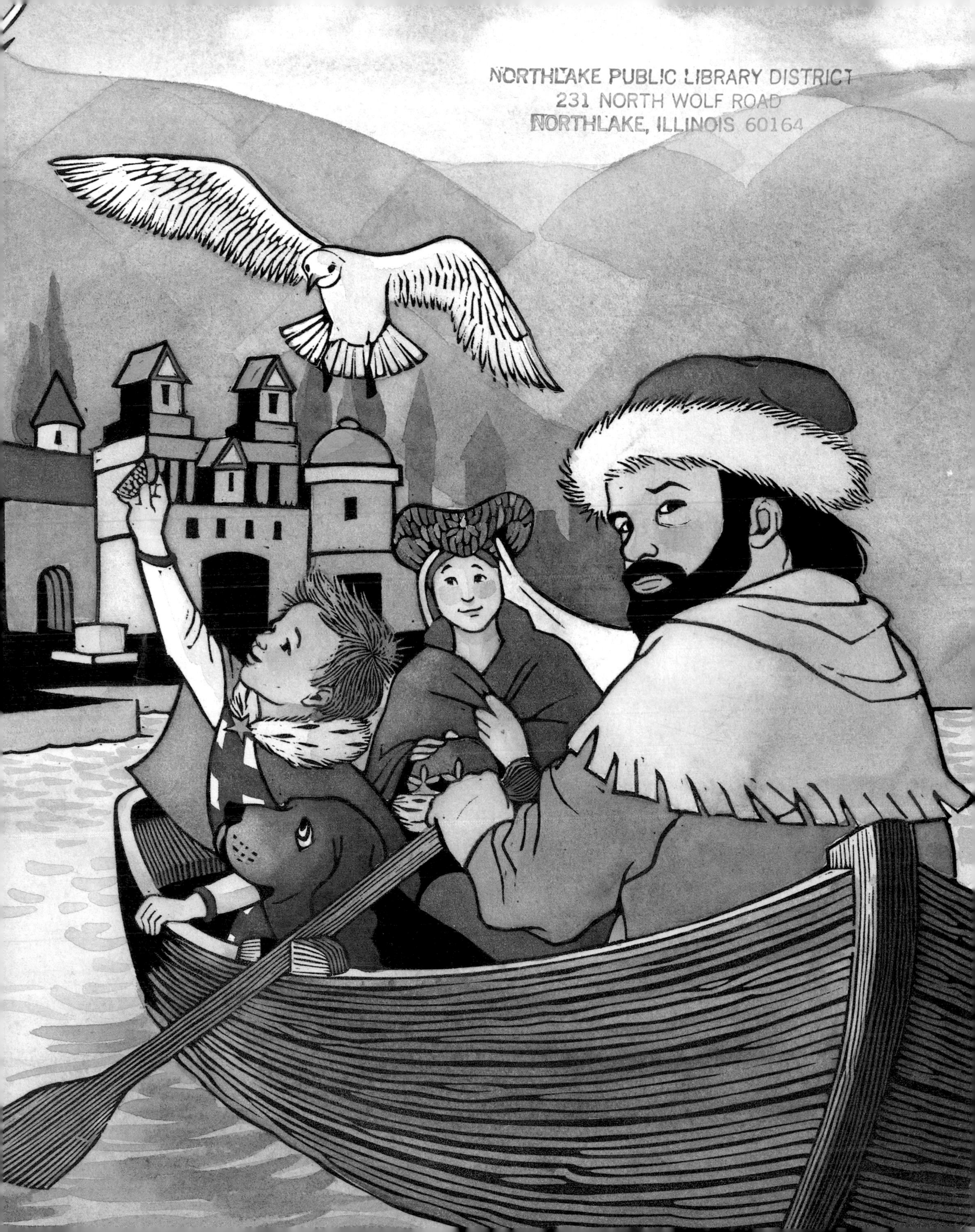

This one is sailing
and that one is moored:
Hark to the song
of the sailors on board!

And see on the steps
  of my palace, the kings

Coming and going
with presents and things!

Now I have done with it,
down let it go!

All in a moment
    the town is laid low.

Block upon block lying scattered and free,
What is there left of my town by the sea?

Yet as I saw it, I see it again,
The kirk and the palace,
   the ships and the men,
And as long as I live,
   and where'er I may be,
I'll always remember my town
   by the sea.